The Angel
and the Soldier Boy

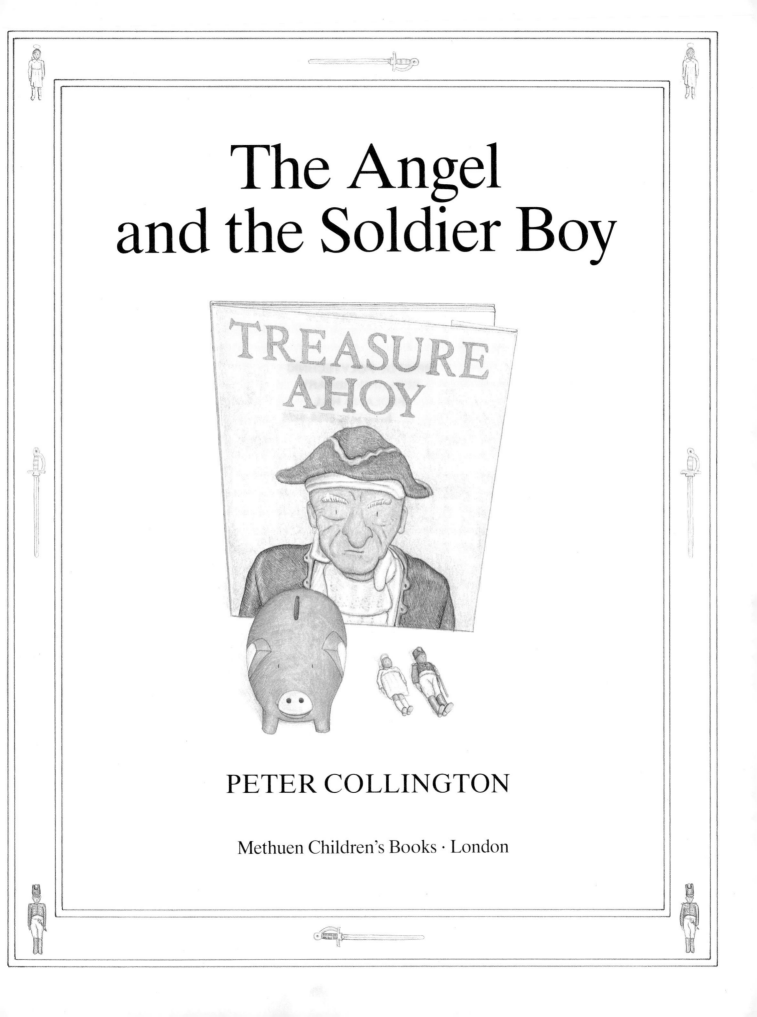

PETER COLLINGTON

Methuen Children's Books · London

For Bonnie and Sasha
Special thanks to Ross and John

First published in Great Britain in 1987
by Methuen Children's Books Ltd
11 New Fetter Lane, London EC4P 4EE
Illustrations copyright © 1987 Peter Collington
Printed in Great Britain
by Hazell Watson & Viney Ltd
Member of the BPCC Group
Aylesbury, Bucks

British Library Cataloguing in Publication Data

Collington, Peter
  The angel and the soldier boy.
  I. Title
  741   PZ7

  ISBN 0-416-96870-8

The artwork is executed in
coloured pencil and water colour on card.

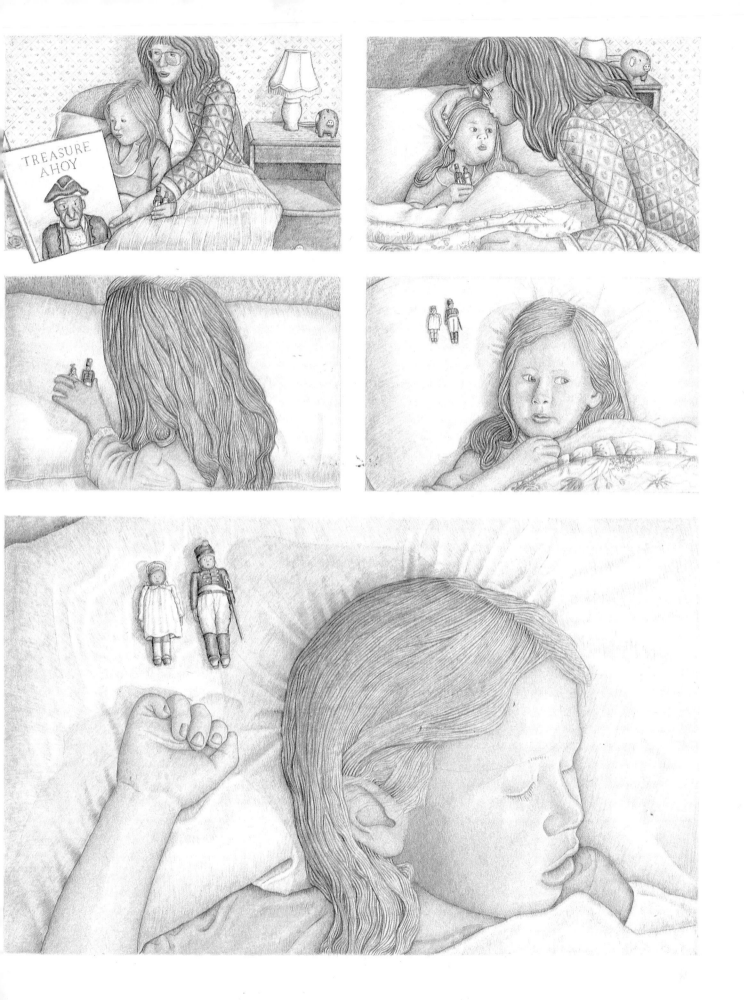

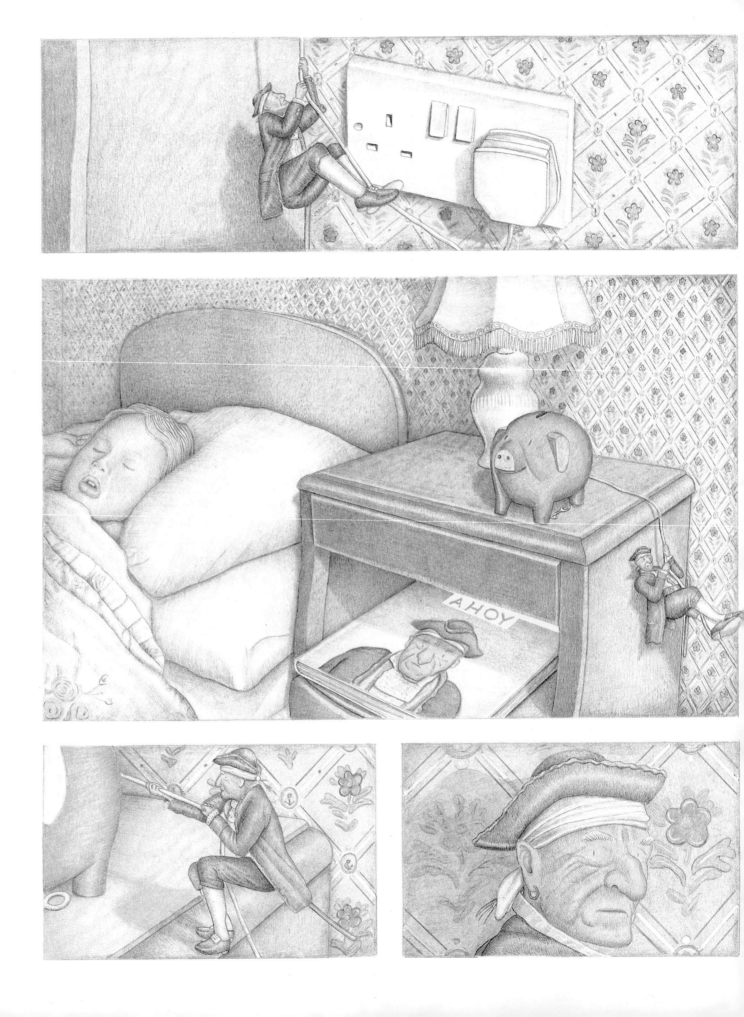

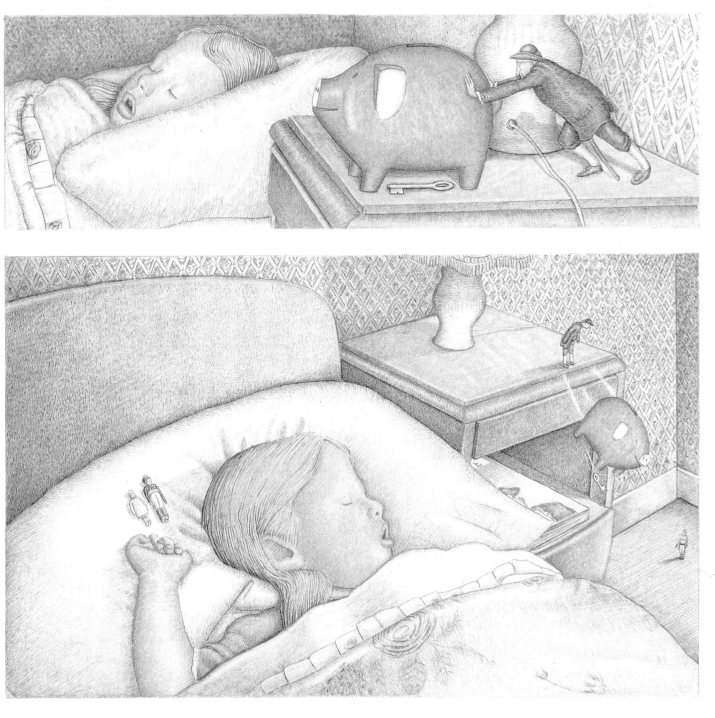

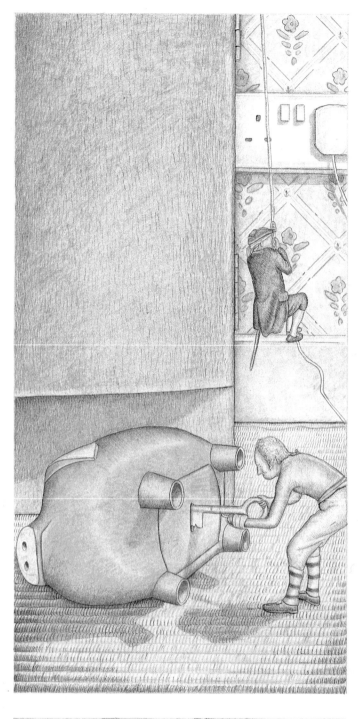
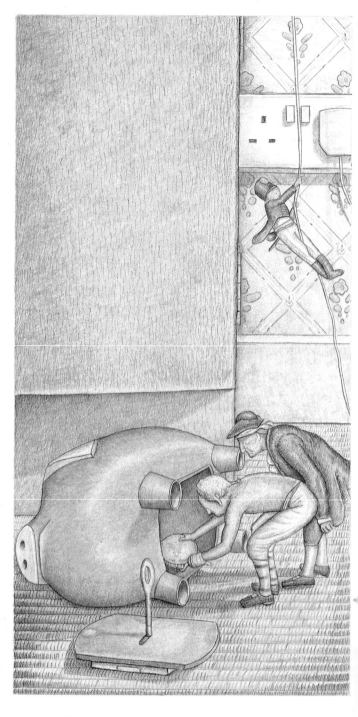

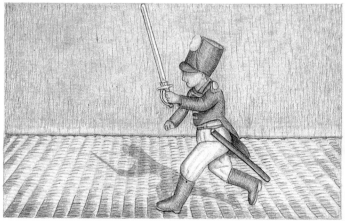

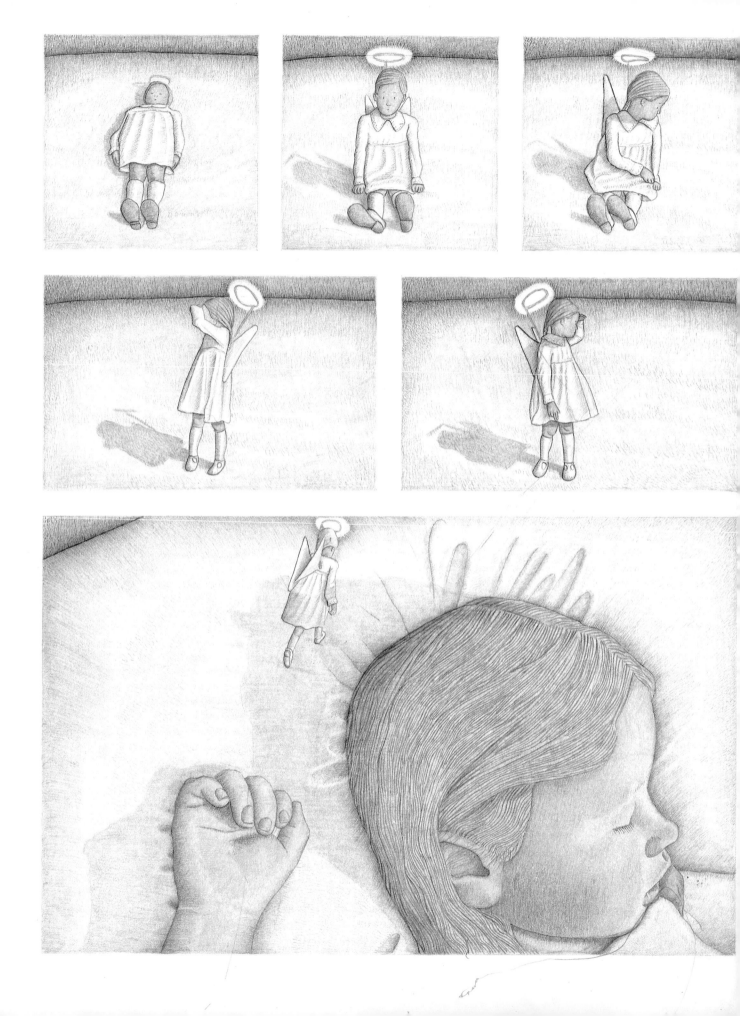

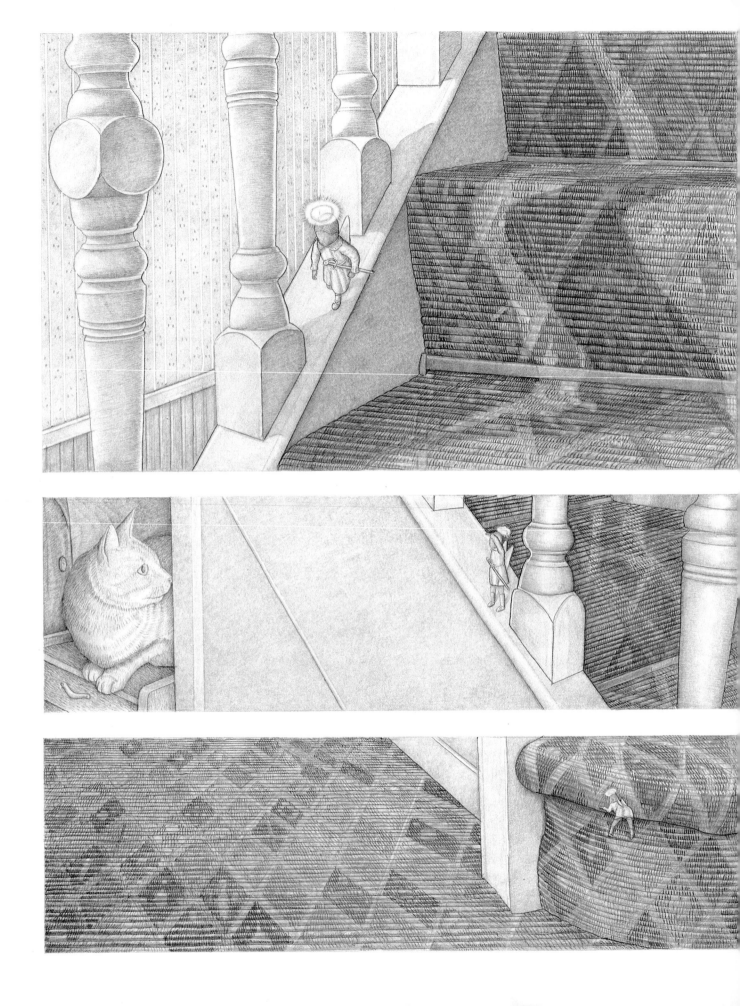

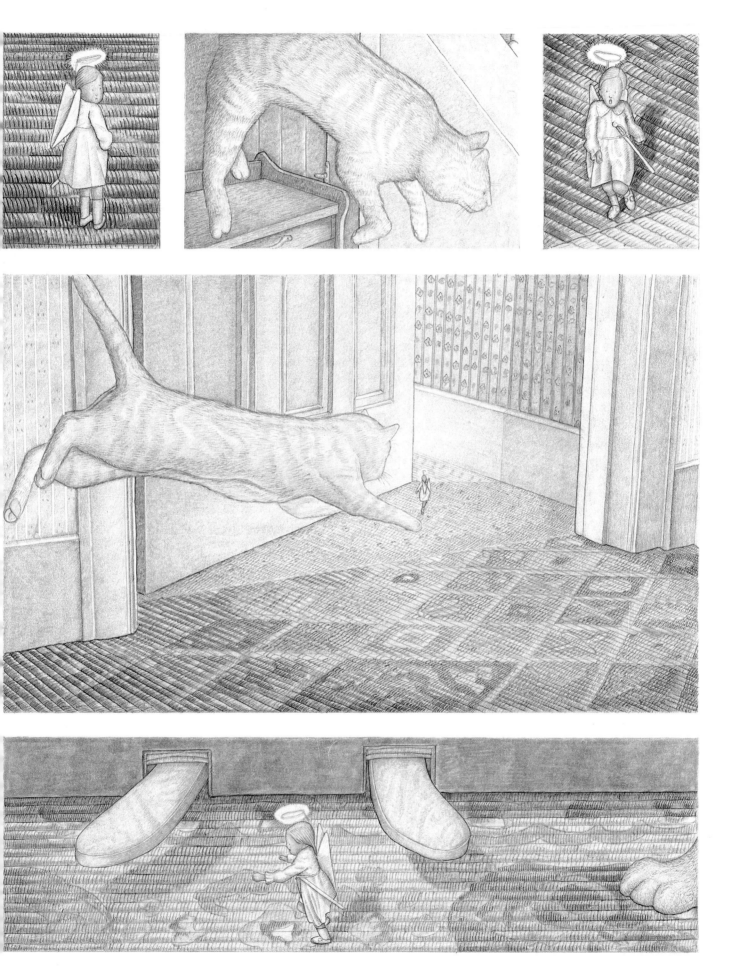

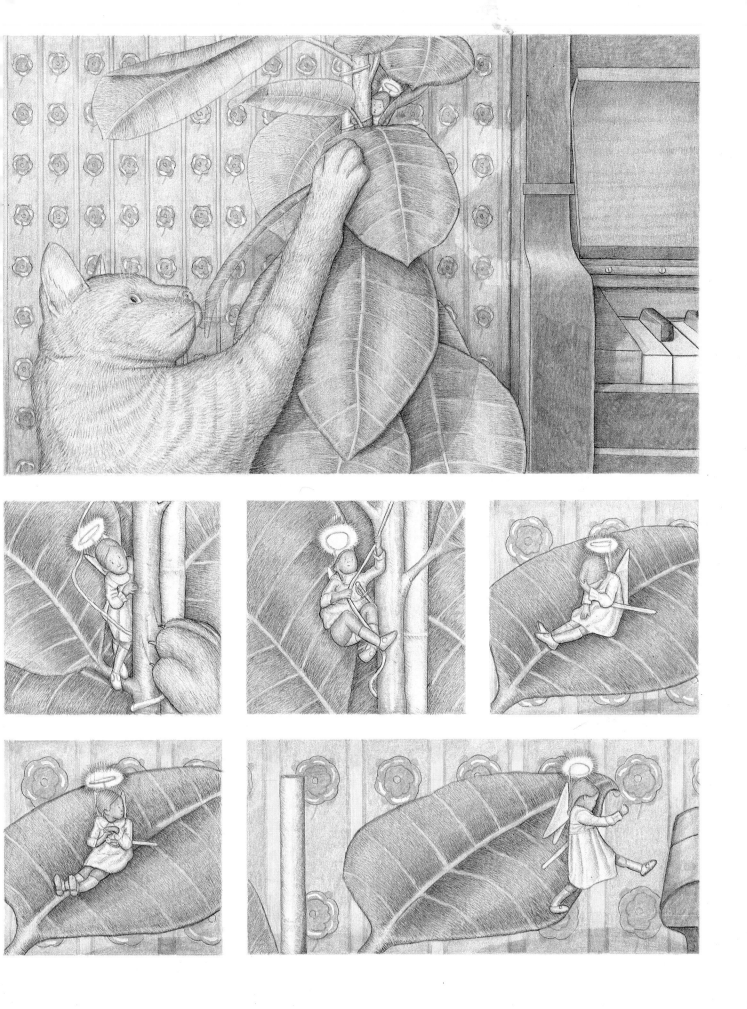

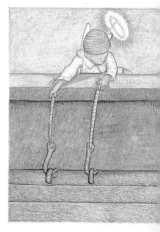

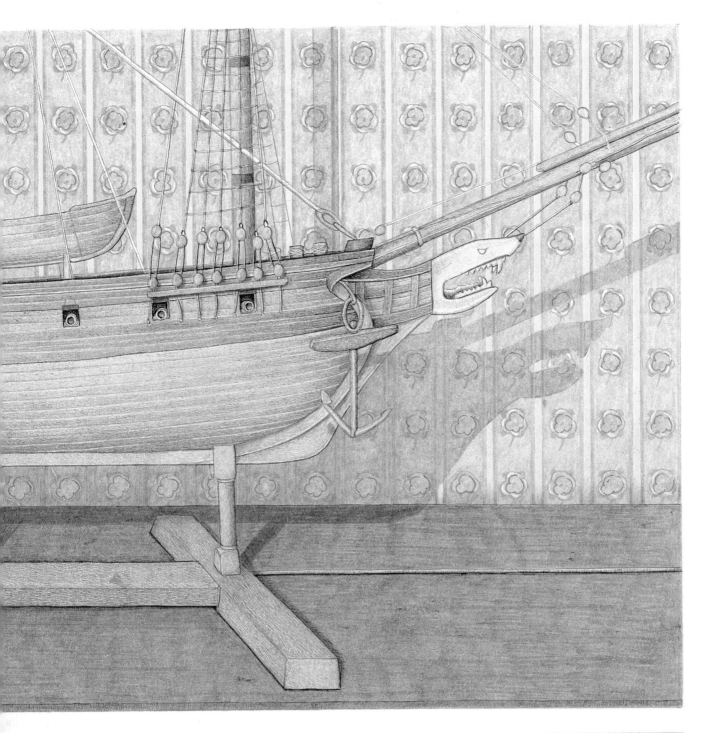

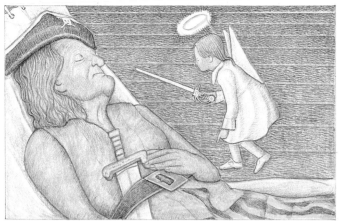

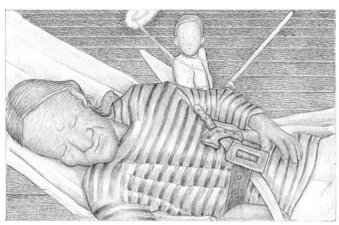

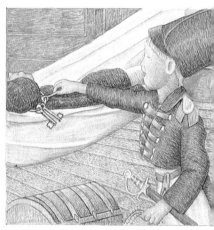

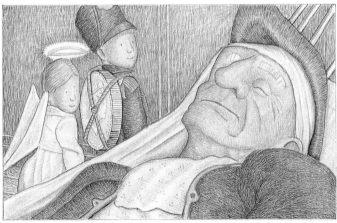